Pebble® Plus
Bilingüe/Bilingual

Animales bebé / Baby Animals

La historia de un conejo bebé /
A Baby Rabbit Story

por/by Jeni Wittrock

Editora consultora/Consulting Editor: Gail Saunders-Smith, PhD

Consultora/Consultant: Marsha A. Sovada, PhD, Bióloga de Investigación de la
Fauna y Flora Silvestre/Research Wildlife Biologist
Northern Prairie Wildlife Research Center
U.S. Geological Survey, Jamestown, North Dakota

CAPSTONE PRESS
a capstone imprint

Busy mother rabbit is building
a nest. Twigs, grass, and
leaves will make a good home
for new baby bunnies.

———————————————

La atareada mamá coneja está haciendo un
nido. Varas, hierbas y hojas harán un buen
hogar para los nuevos conejos bebé.

Soon four tiny bunnies are born.

The wiggly babies are

pinkish-gray and naked.

Brr! Snuggle, bunnies!

They keep each other warm.

Pronto nacen cuatro pequeños conejitos.

Los temblorosos bebés son color gris con

rosa y están desnudos.

¡Brr! ¡Acurrúquense, conejitos!

Se dan calor unos a otros.

Newborn rabbits can't see.

The mother rabbit feeds

her babies milk from her body.

The bunnies grow fast.

_____

Los conejos recién nacidos no pueden ver.

La mamá coneja alimenta a sus bebés con

leche de su cuerpo.

Los conejos bebé crecen rápidamente.

Blink! After three or four days,

the bunnies' eyes open.

Their new fur is slick

and brown.

_____

¡Parpadean! Después de tres o cuatro días,

los conejitos abren los ojos.

Su nuevo pelaje es liso y marrón.

Mom only visits her nest twice
a day. She doesn't stay long.
Predators might see her.
She stays away to keep
her babies safe.

Mamá solo visita su nido dos veces al día.
Ella no se queda mucho tiempo.
Los depredadores podrían verla.
Ella se aleja para mantener a sus
bebés a salvo.

Soon the bunnies begin

to explore. Shh!

Did you hear that?

Little bunny ears perk up

and turn to listen all around.

Pronto los conejitos empiezan a explorar.

¡Shh! ¿Escuchaste eso?

Pequeñas orejitas de conejo se levantan y

giran para escuchar.

Munch, munch, munch.

Three-week-old bunnies eat grass,

weeds, fruit, and vegetables.

Time for a taste of clover!

Cronch, cronch, cronch.

Los conejos bebé de tres semanas de edad

comen pasto, hierbas, fruta y vegetales.

¡Es hora de probar un trébol!

After eating, bunnies groom
fluffy fur. Use your front paws
to clean your face and ears.
Don't forget to wash your paws!

Después de comer, los conejitos se
acicalan su esponjoso pelaje. Usa tus patas
delanteras para limpiar tu cara y tus orejas.
¡No te olvides de lavarte las patitas!

Boing! Boing! Look at me!

The young rabbits spring

straight up in the air.

Let's play all day.

¡Boing! ¡Boing! ¡Mírame!

Los jóvenes conejos saltan en el aire.

Vamos a jugar todo el día.

Bye, mom! At two months old,

bunnies are on their own.

They will find mates and

have families of their own.

¡Adiós, Mamá! A los dos meses de edad,

los conejitos se quedan solos.

Encontrarán pareja y tendrán sus

propias familias.

Glossary

groom—to clean one's fur

mate—a male or female partner of a pair of animals

predator—an animal that hunts and eats other animals

slick—pressed tight to the body

spring—to leap up in the air

wiggly—moving with lots of small motions

Internet Sites

FactHound offers a safe, fun way to find Internet sites related to this book. All of the sites on FactHound have been researched by our staff.

Here's all you do:

Visit *www.facthound.com*

Type in this code: 9781429692205

Glosario

acicalarse—limpiarse su propio pelaje

el depredador—un animal que caza y se come a otros animales

liso—pegado al cuerpo

la pareja—el compañero macho o hembra de un animal

saltar—brincar en el aire

tembloroso—moverse haciendo muchos movimientos pequeños

Sitios de Internet

FactHound brinda una forma segura y divertida de encontrar sitios de Internet relacionados con este libro. Todos los sitios en FactHound han sido investigados por nuestro personal.

Esto es todo lo que tienes que hacer:

Visita *www.facthound.com*

Ingresa este código: 9781429692205

Pebble Plus is published by Capstone Press,
1710 Roe Crest Drive, North Mankato, Minnesota 56003.
www.capstonepub.com

Library of Congress Cataloging-in-Publication Data
Wittrock, Jeni.
[Baby rabbit story. Spanish & English]
La historia de un conejo bebé = a baby rabbit story / por/by Jeni Wittrock ; editora consultora/consulting editor, Gail Saunders-Smith ; consultora/consultant, Marsha A. Sovada.
p. cm.—(Pebble plus bilingue/bilingual: animales bebé/baby animals)
Includes index.
ISBN 978-1-4296-9220-5 (library binding)
ISBN 978-1-62065-332-6 (ebook PDF)
1. Rabbits—Infancy—Juvenile literature. I. Title. II. Title: Baby rabbit story.
QL737.L32.W5818 2013
599.32—dc23   2011050100

Summary: Full-color photographs and simple text describe how baby rabbits grow up.

Editorial Credits
Erika L. Shores, editor; Strictly Spanish, translation services; Ashlee Suker, designer;
   Laura Manthe, bilingual book designer and production specialist; Svetlana Zhurkin, media researcher

Photo Credits
Alamy/Wild Dales Photography/Simon Phillpotts, 19
Getty Images/Jack Milchanowski, 9
iStockphoto/Dieter Spears, cover; Maurice van der Velden, 12–13
Photolibrary/Peter Arnold/Stan Osolinski, 11
Photo Researchers/G. Ronald Austing, 7; Scott Camazine, 4–5
Shutterstock/Graham Taylor, 1, 15; Wayne James, 20–21
Visuals Unlimited/Robert & Jean Pollock, 16–17; Steve Maslowski, 3

The author lovingly dedicates this book to Bunbun, the rabbit who changed it all.

Note to Parents and Teachers

The Animales bebé/Baby Animals series supports national science standards related to life science. This book describes and illustrates baby rabbits. The images support early readers in understanding the text. The repetition of words and phrases helps early readers learn new words. This book also introduces early readers to subject-specific vocabulary words, which are defined in the Glossary section. Early readers may need assistance to read some words and to use the Glossary, Internet Sites, and Index sections of the book.

Printed in the United States of America in North Mankato, Minnesota.
042012   006682CGF12

Index

Índice